FOR EMILE · ELSIE · EMMA

M.R.

FOR DAISY

K.W.

First published 2010 by Walker Books Ltd
87 Vauxhall Walk, London SE11 5HJ

2 4 6 8 10 9 7 5 3 1

Text © 2010 Michael Rosen
Illustrations © 2010 Kevin Waldron

The right of Michael Rosen and Kevin Waldron to be
identified as author and illustrator respectively of this work
has been asserted by them in accordance with the
Copyright, Designs and Patents Act 1988

This book has been typeset in Egyptian Extended

Printed in China

British Library Cataloguing in Publication Data:
a catalogue record for this book is available from
the British Library

ISBN 978-1-4063-1455-7
www.walker.co.uk

# TINY LITTLE FLY

WORDS BY
## MICHAEL ROSEN

PICTURES BY
## KEVIN WALDRON

**WALKER BOOKS**
AND SUBSIDIARIES
LONDON · BOSTON · SYDNEY · AUCKLAND

My oh my,
Tiny Little Fly!

Tiny Little Fly
Sees great big toes...

Tiny Little Fly
Sits on Elephant's nose.

Great Big Elephant
Winks one eye,
Says to himself,
"I'm going to catch that fly!"

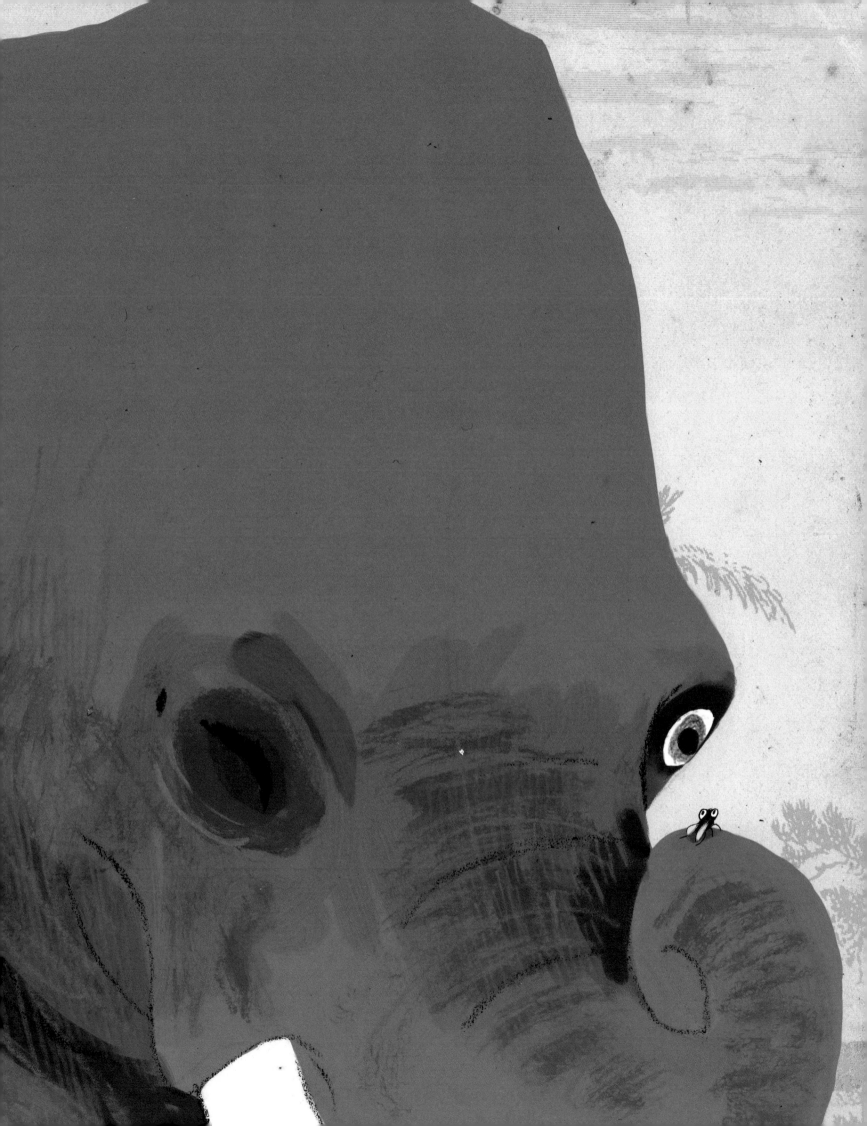

Great Big Elephant
Winks the other eye.

**TRAMP! CRUSH! TRAMP!**

But off flies the fly.

My oh my,
Tiny Little Fly!

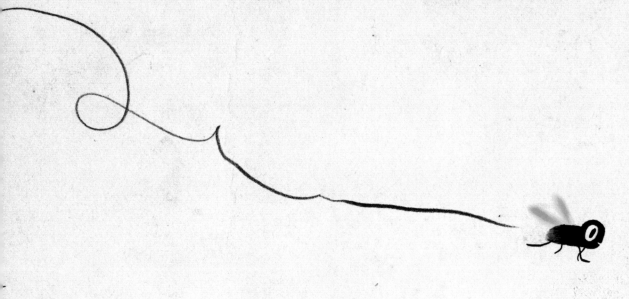

Tiny Little Fly
Says, "What's this here...?

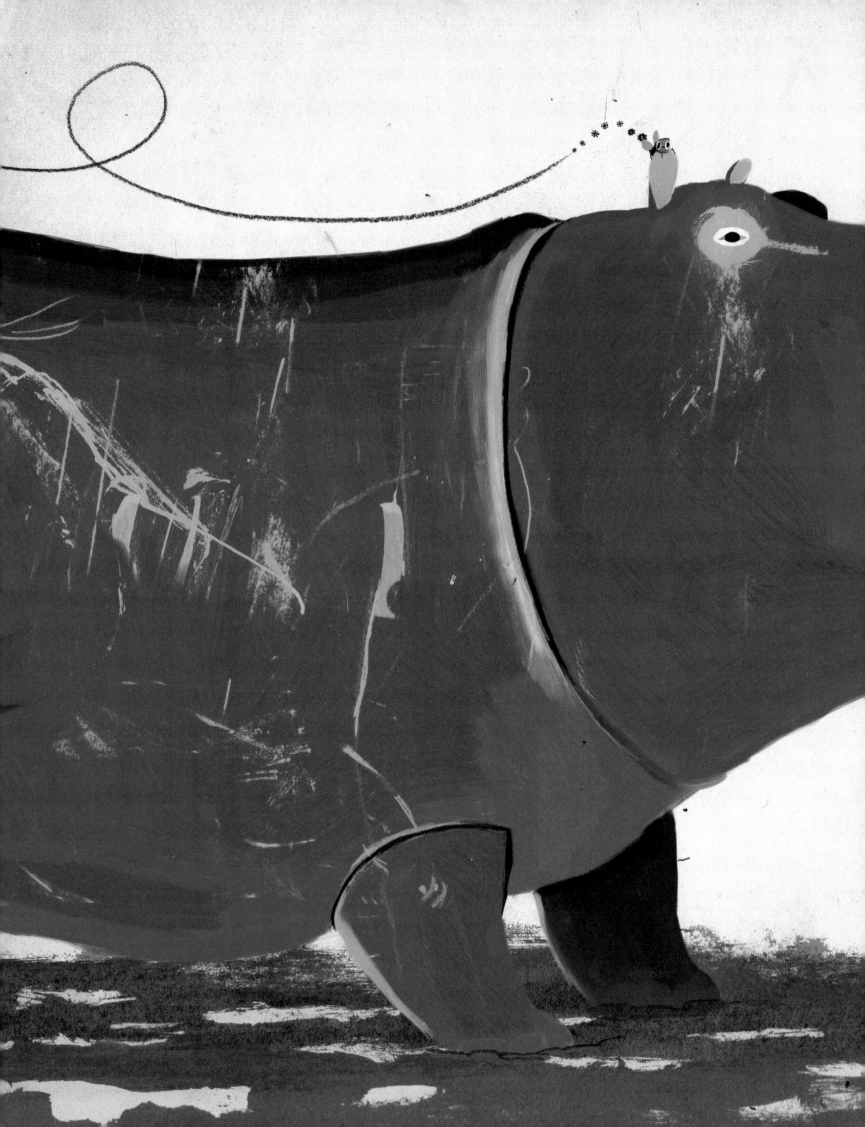

# Great Big Hippo!"
And settles on his ear.

Great Big Hippo winks one eye, says

to himself, "I'm going to catch that fly!"

Great Big Hippo
Winks the other eye.

# ROLL! SQUASH! ROLL!

But off flies the fly.

My oh my,
Tiny Little Fly!

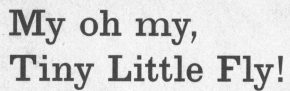

Tiny Little Fly
Sees some stripy paws...

"It's a great big tiger!"
And settles on her claws.

"It's a great big tiger!"

Great Big Tiger winks one eye, says to

herself, "I'm going to catch that fly!"

Great Big Tiger
Winks the other eye.

SWOOP! SNATCH! SWOOP!

But off flies the fly.

Great Big
TRAMP! CRUSH
Great Big
ROLL! SQUASH
Great Big
SWOOP! SNATCH!

And Tiny Little Fly.

*Fly! Fly! Fly!*

# Elephant.

**TRAMP!**

# Hippo.

**ROLL!**

# Tiger.

**SWOOP!**

Tiny Little Fly,
Winks one eye...

"See you
all soon.
Bye,
everyone,
bye!"